KU-633-113

This Book Belongs to

<u>memphis</u>

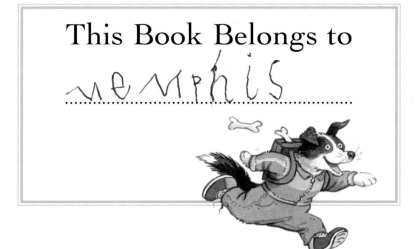

Published by Fernleigh Books
1A London Road, Enfield
Middlesex, EN2 6BN
www.fernleigh.co.uk

Cat's Pyjamas is an imprint of Fernleigh Books
Text copyright © 2009 Fernleigh Books
Illustrations copyright © 2009 Peter Stevenson
All rights reserved
ISBN 978-1-906293-67-3
Printed in China

Five Minute Collection

Bedtime Farm Tales

Miss Long Legs Wins

Felicity the foal was fed up with all the other farm animals teasing her.

"Look at those long wobbly legs," they laughed. "You'll never be able to enter the roller skate race at school with legs like that!"

Her mother bought her two lovely pairs of skates – one for her front legs and one for the back. But every time she tried to skate, her long legs got in a tangle.

"Keep on practising," said her father. "You'll soon get the hang of it."

The day of the race arrived. The headmaster, Mr Cockerel, lifted the starting flag and they were off. At first Felicity went slowly, but then she began to feel more confident. Soon, her long legs had taken her past the leader, and she skated home the winner. She was so happy!

"I love my long legs," she cried. "Perhaps one day I'll even be a race horse!"

A Very, Very Old Hat

One spring, Farmer Giles looked at his old felt hat. It was starting to look a little battered. The crown had holes in it and the rim was very bent. It was very, very old, and not fit for wearing, even to do the ploughing.

"I ought to throw it away and buy a new one," he said to himself, hanging it up in the barn, "but I'd rather it went to a new home."

As the days became warmer, Mr and Mrs Robin began to look for a nest site. "This is perfect," Mr Robin said excitedly when he found the old hat. They lined it with twigs and soft feathers. Then Mrs Robin laid six pale green eggs, and settled down to keep them warm.

A few weeks later, the eggs hatched. Mr and Mrs Robin were kept very busy, bringing food to their hungry family! They didn't even notice Farmer Giles come to throw away his old hat.

"Bless my soul!" he smiled. "That hat is still useful after all. It belongs to the birds now."

Toby's Secret Talent

Toby the tomcat looked like a typical farm cat. He had long tomcat claws, and sharp white tomcat teeth that gleamed when he smiled. He swaggered across the farmyard by day, flexing his large tomcat muscles, looking very fierce indeed. All the birds and mice were frightened of him!

But Toby wasn't a typical farm cat at all. In fact, he had a very unusual secret.

Next time you visit the farmyard at night, when all the other animals are asleep, and you are very quiet, you might just hear a rather odd sound that goes TAPPITY TAP TAP, TAPPITY TAP TAP. For when night falls, Toby the typical tomcat likes to tap dance. Now that isn't very typical at all, is it?

I'm Bigger Than You!

Charlie the chick was bigger, greedier and bossier than all the other chicks. At mealtimes, Charlie would push the others out of the way and gobble up as much corn as he could.

"I'm bigger than you," he would say. "I need more food!"

One day, Charlie found a trail of corn running across the yard, from a tiny hole in the farmer's basket.

"I can have this all to myself," he thought greedily. So he gobbled his way along the trail, until BUMP! He walked straight into a great big goose.

"Keep away from my corn!" hissed the big bossy bird, pecking at him. "I'm bigger than you. I need more food!"

Charlie did not wait to argue. He ran off across the farmyard as fast as his legs would carry him. After that, Charlie didn't feel quite so big or bossy anymore.

The Holidays Are Here!

Sam the puppy couldn't wait for the end of term.

"School's boring!" he said to his mum. "I shall have two whole weeks off to play soon. I shall play all day long, from the minute I wake up until I go to bed."

On the last day of term, he came bounding home from school, his lunchbox on his back and the biggest ever smile on his face.

"I'm home!" he cried. "Now it's time to have some fun."

On the first morning of the holidays he chased the ducks and chickens, then swam in the stream. On the second day, he followed the farmer's wife down to the village to do some shopping, and on the third day he watched the farmer doing his haymaking. By the fourth day, he was feeling a bit lonely – and very bored.

"When does school start again, Mum?" he asked. "It's so boring at home!"

A Simple Mistake To Make

Posy the cat was taking her kittens for their first outing.

"Stay close to me!" she told the little brown fuzzy balls of fur.

But Joe, who was the bravest of all the kittens, caught sight of Rachel the duck waddling past with a trail of little ducklings. The ducklings were little, brown and fuzzy, just like him.

"Maybe they are another cat family," he thought, joining the line. "I'll follow them and see what happens."

When they came to the pond, Rachel the duck hopped straight into the water, closely followed by her ducklings – and Joe the kitten, too.

"Help!" cried Joe, scrambling out of the cold water and shaking himself dry. He watched the little ducklings bob and dive on the pond.

"They might be fuzzy and brown," he decided, "but they're definitely NOT just like me." And off he scampered to the safety of his mum.

The Daisy Chain Rescue

One day, four new cows arrived at the farm. Three of them were called Daisy, but the fourth had a very unusual name.

"I am no ordinary cow like you," she proudly told the others. "My name is Eglantine." And off she walked to the other end of the field.

What Eglantine didn't know was that it was very muddy at the other end of the field. One minute she was happily munching clover – the next she was stuck in the mud.

"Help!" she mooed.

Quick as a flash, the three Daisies sprang into action. Daisy One caught Eglantine by the tail, Daisy Two grabbed Daisy One's tail, and Daisy Three grabbed Daisy Two's tail. Together, they pulled Eglantine out of the mud.

"I'm so sorry I called you ordinary!" apologised Eglantine. "It's not every day I am rescued by a Daisy chain!"

Picnic Time for Poppy

One morning, Poppy the pig was taking a mud bath when Charlie the calf popped his head over the wall.

"Don't forget the picnic," he said.

"Bother!" grunted Poppy. "That means Mum will make me clean myself up. I'd rather stay here in the mud." So she ignored Charlie, and carried on getting mucky. There was nothing she liked better!

The farmyard grew quiet. Poppy's tummy began to rumble. She thought of the other animals eating all the lovely picnic food, and wished she had got ready in time.

Just then, it began to rain. "I'm in luck!" cried Poppy. The rain quickly washed away all the mud. Soon, Poppy was as pink as a pig can be again and she trotted off to the barn where the others were sheltering.

"Come on!" she cried. "The rain has stopped. It's time to eat!"
And it wasn't long before everyone was enjoying a wonderful picnic.

Mr Fix It Does it Again

Cosmo the kid's dad could fix anything – clocks, radios, bicycles, you name it, he could fix it.

One day, Cosmo was playing with a big red balloon when it landed on a sharp thorn and popped with a loud bang. Cosmo wasn't sad: he knew his dad could fix it. He could fix anything. But he was in for a surprise.
"I'm afraid I can't fix it," said Dad, sadly. "Some things just can't be fixed."

Cosmo began to cry, but suddenly Mr Goat said, "I know what I can fix, though – your sad face." And he gave Cosmo a brand new red balloon and a big kiss. Cosmo was happy again – perhaps his dad could fix anything after all!

Jossie's Old Bicycle

Jossie the pony had an old bicycle that needed painting. The trouble was, Jossie just couldn't decide which colour to paint it.

"Paint it green," said Maisie the sheep, "green like the grass - delicious!"

"No, no, no," oinked Petunia the pig, "pink is best – pigs are pink!"

"Blue!" cried Mr Duck, "like the colour of my pond."

"It must be yellow," argued Lottie the duckling, "just like my soft feathers."

No-one could agree, and Jossie was very confused. Suddenly, he had an idea. He went off with his paintbrush, without a word to anyone.

What a surprise when Jossie returned to show off his newly painted bike! Its handlebars were green, the pedals were pink, the seat was blue and the wheels were bright yellow. Now everyone was happy!

Tilly Turkey Stays Up Late

Mrs Turkey was calling her chicks.

"Gobble, gobble," she said. "It's bedtime."

But Tilly wouldn't listen. She just carried on playing. Mrs Turkey held out her wing, and all the other chicks scrambled underneath. Soon they were fast asleep. But Tilly just kept on playing.

There was a rumble of thunder, and a flash of lightning and it began to rain. Tilly ran to hide under her mother's wing, but she was cold and wet, and the other chicks were not pleased.

"Go away," they said, pushing her back into the rain. "You're making us wet."

"Please let me in," begged Tilly.

"It's a good job I've got two wings," smiled her mother, lifting her other wing to shelter Tilly. "Perhaps you'll do as you're told next time."

But Tilly didn't hear her. She was already fast asleep.

A Room With A View

Penny the pig's sty was the envy of all the other farm animals. It was warm and cosy, and painted bright blue. But Penny wasn't happy with her home. She wanted a view.

"It's no problem for you," she told Harry the carthorse. "You're so big and tall, you can see for miles from your stable door."

Harry thought hard about what Penny had said. He decided to surprise her with a solution to her problem.

The next day, while Penny was out, he found a small wooden chair in the barn and fixed it to the roof of Penny's sty. Next, he nailed an old piece of fencing to the roof to make a ladder.

When Penny came home she was delighted. She had a view over the whole farm!

Lonely Tommy Toad

Tommy the toad lived in the farm pond. One day, the farmer's children, Lucy and Jack, were fishing in the pond, when they caught Tommy in their net.

"Ugh!" cried Lucy, looking at Tommy. "What a horrible, brown, lumpy thing!" Tommy leapt out of the net.

"I wish I wasn't so ugly," he sighed, looking at his reflection in the pond. "No one will ever love me."

Tommy decided to hide away at the bottom of the pond. But as he swam down through the water, he passed … another toad. She was lumpy and brown, just like him.

"Hello," she said. "I'm new to this pond. My name is Priscilla."

"Hello," gasped Tommy. "I think you're lovely!"

"And you are the most handsome toad I have even seen," replied Priscilla shyly. And they hopped off – happily ever after!

Maddy's Special Letter

Early in the morning, Mr Duck the postman delivered the post to Acorn Farm. And every morning, Maddy the donkey would trot down to the gate with the other animals to meet him.

"Is there a letter for me?" she asked.

"Sorry! Not today," he would reply.

Day after day went by, but poor Maddy never got a single letter. In the end, she didn't even bother to ask. She just watched sadly as the other animals collected their post. Then, one day, Mr Duck suddenly shouted, "Hey, Maddy! Don't you want your letter?"

Maddy's heart missed a beat. "For me?" she cried.

"All the way from Australia," said Mr Duck.

Maddy tore open the envelope. "My sister is coming to visit!" she shouted.

And Maddy was even more pleased when the animals all agreed that it was the most exciting letter ever delivered to Acorn Farm.

Barney Gets It Right

Barney the bull was the biggest animal on the farm. He was also the clumsiest. He didn't mean to tread on the other animals' toes, or break things – he was just so big and heavy.

One day, Barney was walking along day-dreaming, when THUMP! he bumped into Mrs Hen's apple tree. All the apples fell to the ground.

"Oh dear," cried Barney. "Whatever shall I do?"

He was just wondering if he could glue all the apples back on the tree, when Mrs Hen came hurrying out of the henhouse.

"Thank you for picking all the apples," she clucked. "I couldn't reach them."

That night, as a reward, Mrs Hen baked Barney the biggest apple pie he'd EVER seen – big enough to feed even the biggest animal on the farm!

Bessie Flies Too Far

Bessie the bee was so busy collecting pollen, she didn't notice how far she had wandered away from home – until it was too late.

"Where am I?" worried Bessie, looking around. All she could see were flowers.

Just then, Chirpy the chicken came hopping by.

"I live in the orchard," Bessie told Chirpy, "but I can't find my way home."

"Don't worry!" replied Chirpy. "I'll show you."

So Bessie buzzed along behind Chirpy. They soon reached Bessie's beehive in the orchard.

Suddenly, a stray dog bounded up. It barked loudly at Chirpy.

"BUZZZZ off!" cried Bessie, zooming round the dog's ears. The dog didn't need telling twice! He stopped barking, and ran off at once.

"Thank you for rescuing me!" said Chirpy.

"One good turn deserves another," smiled Bessie. "Now, won't you stay for tea? I've got lots of delicious honey." How could Chirpy refuse?

Tiger Puss, Tiger Puss

Matilda was a tiny kitten with claws like needles! Every time her owner Daisy tried to pick her up, she scratched her and spat.

One day, Matilda escaped her basket, and scampered off to look for somebody to scratch. It wasn't long before she spotted the carthorse. But he was so big, he didn't even see Matilda, and nearly stood on her.

"Help!" cried Matilda, scampering away.

"Are you all right?" asked a tiny mouse.

"Of course!" hissed Matilda, pushing out her claws and trying to look fierce. But the little mouse smiled. "Don't be afraid," she said. "I won't hurt you."

"But I might!" snarled a voice. Matilda looked up in alarm. It was an enormous farm cat.

Suddenly, Matilda was scooped up in the air.

"Poor kitty!" said Daisy, shooing away the farm cat and stroking Matilda's fur.
Matilda purred with relief. And she never scratched Daisy, or anyone else, ever again!

Eight Poor, Sore Piglets

It was a very hot day. Mrs Pig's piglets were snoozing in the sty.

"I'm just popping out," she told them. "Mind you stay in the shade while I'm gone. Your skin is pink and you're not very hairy, so you could get sunburnt." As soon as she was gone, Percy, the naughtiest of the eight piglets, scampered over to a patch of sunlight in the middle of the sty.

"Come on," he cried. "Let's play chase."

Soon, the piglets were having a wonderful time chasing each other into the shade and back again. It was a very tiring game. One by one, the little piglets fell asleep – in the sun!

When Mrs Pig arrived home she found eight very sore, sunburnt little piglets.

"I told you to stay out of the sun!" she scolded. But she took pity on them and rubbed special soothing cream on their sore backs. That's what mums are for!

Hunker's Secret Weapon

Hunker was a huge bouncy puppy with enormous paws and a very waggy tail. Sometimes, he wagged it so hard, he would knock the farmer's two little boys right over – but Timmy and Tommy didn't mind. They loved Hunker, and often fell asleep with their heads on his tummy.

"What a big softie Hunker is," their mother would smile.

One day, a naughty fox came to the farm and stole a chicken. As he crept away, who should he bump into but Hunker.

"Hello!" grinned the bouncy puppy, and he wagged his tail so hard that it knocked the fox right over. The fox dropped the chicken at once and ran away.

"Dad!" shouted Timmy and Tommy. "Hunker caught a thief!"

"Good pup!" said the farmer, patting Hunker. "You might be a big softie, but you'll be a fine guard dog one day."

Stranger In The Pond

Danny the duckling was gliding over the duckpond when he noticed a strange green creature swimming by.

"What a funny fish," he thought, and he hurried off to tell his brother and sister, Toby and Lily, what he had just seen.

"Look!" he quacked, as the strange green fish jumped out of the pond.

"Fish don't jump!" said Toby.

"Or have legs!" added Lily. So they went and told their mum all about it.

Mrs Frog burst out laughing. "That's Freddie the frog,' she said. "The last time I saw him, he was just a tiny tadpole wriggling in the reeds. Why don't you ask him if he would like to play?"

So Toby and Lily did.

"I'd love to," croaked Freddie. And they all spent the rest of the afternoon playing a new game Freddie taught them – leapfrog!

Cedric Finds His Voice

Cedric was the biggest chick in the henhouse, and he was getting bigger every day. His legs were getting longer, his feathers smoother, and he was growing a fine red cockscomb on his head.

"Soon, I'll make the loudest noise in the farmyard," he told everyone. Then he threw back his head … and made an odd sort of gurgling sound.

Then, one morning Cedric got up just as dawn was breaking. He felt rather peculiar, so he strutted out into the yard and climbed on top of the wall. He threw back his head … and crowed at the top of his voice!

"COCK-A-DOODLE-DOO!"

Once he had started, Cedric just couldn't stop. "COCK-A-DOODLE-DOO!" he crowed, over and over.

The other animals crowded round, chattering excitedly.

"Cedric's grown up!" they cried. Cedric felt very proud.

Finding A Favourite Place

One day, the kittens were talking about the places they had discovered around the farm.

"My favourite is the barn," said Blackie. "I love hiding in the straw."

"I like the yard best," said Teeny. "It's fun playing with the chicks. What about you, Splodge?"

But Splodge didn't know. "I haven't found one yet," he said. And he crept off, feeling rather embarrassed.

"How do you find a favourite place?" he wondered.

Then Splodge had an idea. He scrambled up a tall apple tree, and scratched his claws on the rough bark. Then he stretched out on a warm sunny branch and looked down at the farm below.

"I'm sure to spot a favourite place from up here," he said. And that's when it came to him.

"Silly me!" he grinned. "I know my favourite place. It's right here – where I can see everything!"

Happy Birthday Dilly!

It was Dilly the duckling's birthday, and she was having a swimming party for all her duckling friends. But Dilly was feeling sad.

Now, you might wonder why, but the reason was simple. Ducklings love rain – especially if they are going swimming – and the sun was shining that morning.

"No-one will want to come now," sniffed Dilly.

"Cheer up," comforted her mum. "It still might rain. Let's see what the other animals think." But nobody knew for sure.

Then Mrs Duck saw Mrs Cow lying down in the field. All the other cows were lying down, too.

"What's the matter?" she asked. "Are you feeling unwell?"

"Moo, no!" replied Mrs Cow, laughing. "Cows always lie down when it's going to rain."

That afternoon it rained and rained – and Dilly's party was a great success.

"Clever Mrs Cow," she quacked.

A Very Special Cow

Buttercup the cow was very bored.

"There must be something more exciting to do than eat grass and make milk all day," she sighed, fluttering her eyelashes, and admiring her pretty little hooves.

"Nonsense!" mooed her mother. "Making milk is what cows do best."

"But I want to be special," sighed Buttercup. "I want to be noticed!"

The next day while the cows were being milked, a big black limousine drew up, and a man wearing a big hat jumped out. He pointed at Buttercup.

"Oh, what lovely long eyelashes and pretty feet," he cried. "You are perfect for my new film. Come with me, Buttercup, and I'll make you a star!"

And do you know what? He did! He took Buttercup to his television studio where she was tested on camera, and now she's a star of the small screen! The next time you see a cow on television, look closely at her long eyelashes and dainty hooves. It's probably Buttercup, a very special cow!

Laurie Learns Her Lesson

Laurie the lamb spent hours gazing at her reflection in the pond. She never joined in the other lambs' games.

"I don't want to get muddy," she told them, turning up her pretty little nose.

One day, as Laurie was gazing in the water, she caught sight of a little white lamb skipping by, every bit as lovely as herself.

"Hello," she said, spinning round to talk to her. But as Laurie turned she slipped and fell headlong into the pond. SPLOSH!

"Oh, dear, look at Laurie," cried the other lambs, trying hard not to laugh. Laurie looked at her reflection again.

"I look like a haystack!" she gasped, but then she started to giggle. All the others joined in. Laurie never wasted time staring into the water again. She was having too much fun laughing and having fun with her friends.

Patch Saves The Hens

Early one morning, Patch was snoozing in his warm kennel when suddenly he awoke with a start! The hens in the henhouse were making a dreadful racket. Patch sniffed the air. He could smell a fox! Quick as a flash, he rushed to the henhouse.

"Leave those chicken alone!" he barked, chasing after the fox and growling fiercely. The fox did not need telling twice. He took one look at Patch, and ran off with his tail between his legs.

At that moment, the farmer arrived, still wearing his dressing gown.

"All safe now, ladies!" he said to the hens. "You can go back to bed now. That fox won't bother you again."

When Patch awoke the next day, he sniffed the morning air.

And what did he smell this time? A big juicy bone outside his kennel. It was a "Thank you very much!" from the farmer.

It's Raining Flowers!

Natalie and Joe were looking forward to their birthday picnic.

"If it's fine, Uncle Billy said he will set off some fireworks," said Natalie. "I do hope it doesn't rain!"

At that moment, Uncle Billy arrived. "I've brought the fireworks," he said. "Are you ready?"

Natalie and Joe nodded. "Do you think it will rain?" they asked.

"I hope so!" replied Uncle Billy, winking at them.

The twins looked at each other and frowned. What did he mean?

While Natalie and Joe prepared the picnic, Uncle Billy picked some flowers. Then he brought out the fireworks – but he wouldn't let the twins see what he did with them.

WHOOSH! A rocket shot into the air, lifting with it a bunch of colourful flowers. As the rocket burst into stars, a shower of colourful flowers rained down.

"WOW!" gasped the twins. "I hope it rains all night!"

Too Much Food For Hattie

Pattie the pig shared a sty with a much bigger pig called Hattie. They got on very well – apart from one thing. Hattie was very greedy. When mealtime came, she gobbled up all the best food, and left poor Pattie with potato peelings.

"It's not fair!" grumbled Pattie. "What about me?"

"I'm the biggest pig," boomed Hattie. "So I need more food!"

One day, the pigs' food arrived – topped with sticky red jam.

"Yummy!' cried Hattie, pushing Pattie aside and gobbling it up. She didn't notice a big wasp sitting on the jam.

"Buzzz!" said the wasp angrily, and it stung Hattie – right on the end of her nose.

"Ouch!" oinked Hattie. "Why did it sting me?"

"Maybe it didn't want to share the jam," said Pattie.

"But that's greedy!" exclaimed Hattie. Then she blushed, as she realised what she had said. After that, Hattie always shared with her friend!

Rover To The Rescue

Mrs Sheep had lost her little lamb, Lily.

"I only turned my back for a minute," she told Paddy the goat in a worried voice. "She's only a baby too. What can I do?"

"I have an idea," replied Paddy. He ran to where Rover the sheepdog was sleeping in the sun.

"Come quickly," he told Rover. "You must help us find Lily the lamb."

"But I round up sheep," woofed Rover. "I don't know how to find them. I'm not a bloodhound!" He wanted to help though, so he put his nose to the ground and began to sniff. Suddenly, he took an extra large sniff, and raced off.

A few moments later, Mrs Sheep heard a loud woof, then the sound of bleating as Rover chased the little lamb back home.

"I knew you could do it, Rover," said Paddy. "You should feel proud of yourself." And do you know what? Rover did!

I've Lost My Mummy!

Tiny the duckling sat at the edge of the farmyard and tried very hard not to cry.

"I want my mummy!" she sniffed. "If only I could fly, I could look down from the air and find her. But my wings are too small."

"Maybe I could teach you," said Pippin the pig hopefully. "I'm sure you only have to flap your wings. Why don't you give it a try?"

So Tiny hopped onto the fence and flapped her downy wings. For a moment she rose high into the air, hovered for a moment … but then she fell and landed in the pond with a splash!

"Tiny!" cried Pippin, peering into the water. "Are you alright?"

Then he heard Tiny's voice. "Pippin! I've found my mummy!"

And there was Tiny, paddling in the water with her mother and all her brothers and sisters. "I might not be able to fly yet," she cried, "but I can swim!"

Playing Follow My Leader

"We're going up to the hill to graze," Mrs Sheep told her lambs one spring day. "Make sure you follow each other's tail or you might get lost.

Jed the sheepdog rounded them up and the farmer led the way. But Lester the lamb had other ideas. Halfway up the steep track, he thought he'd skip off and explore on his own.

"Come back here!" called his mother, but he wouldn't listen. After a few minutes he looked around and couldn't see anyone anywhere.

"Oh dear!" wailed Lester, "I wish I'd listened to Mum."

Just then, he saw Jed racing over the top of the hill towards him. He had never been so glad to see the bossy sheepdog in his life!

"Come on," Jed barked. "It's time to play follow my leader!"

And this time, Lester did.

Pearl The Proud Sheep

Pearl the sheep loved her soft curly coat. So when spring came, and the farmer announced it was time to shear the sheep, she was not pleased.

"I don't want a haircut," she said firmly. "Even if it's getting hot."

"But our wool is used to make cardigans and jumpers," said her sister.

"I don't care," replied Pearl. "My coat is far too fine for that."

She begged and pleaded so much that finally the farmer gave in.

"Very well," he said. "You may keep your coat. I hope you'll be happy in it!"

Soon the summer came. The sun was hot and bright.

"I feel so hot and sticky," complained Pearl. "I wish I could take my coat off!"

"I thought you wanted to keep it," said her sister.

"I am silly!" admitted Pearl. "Next spring, I will remember how hot I am now, and I'll be first in the queue for a haircut!"

Cheeky Goes Swimming

Cheeky was Molly the hen's most mischievous little chick. One day he was playing hide and seek with his friends Paddles and Emmy the ducklings when their mother called them for lunch. His two little friends hopped in the pond and swam off home.

Cheeky watched them go. "That looks fun," he thought, and paddled off after them into the pond.

"Brrr! It's cold!" he shivered. Suddenly he began to sink.

"Help!" he cried. He had never been so frightened!

Then he felt something nudge him back on to the bank. It was Emmy and Paddles' mummy.

"You silly chick," she said, ruffling his wet feathers. "Only ducklings can swim, my dear, not chicks."

At that moment, Molly clucked over and bundled him safely under her wing to dry.

"Mummy, will you always keep me dry? I don't like wet so much!" said Cheeky.

Charlie's Alarm Clock

"You are late again, Charlie!" said his teacher one morning.

"I'm sorry," said Charlie.

"What you need is an alarm clock," said the teacher, and he was right. So when school finished, Charlie went to buy one.

The next morning, the alarm clock's loud bell woke Charlie with a start.

"Hooray!" he shouted. "I won't be late today!" He quickly ran to school.

"I'm half an hour early," said Charlie proudly, when he bumped into his teacher on the way.

"Well done!" smiled his teacher. "But it's Saturday today – there's no school!" Charlie blushed.

"Never mind," said his teacher. "At least you were early today." And he gave Charlie a big ice cream as a reward.

Who Owns The Egg?

It was bedtime and Flim and Flam were arguing.

"It's mine!" shrieked one.

"No, it's mine!" squawked the other.

"What on earth is going on?" asked Rory the Rooster.

"She's stolen my egg!" said Flim.

"No, she's stolen my egg!" said Flam. And the two silly hens began to push and squabble again, as they both tried to sit on the egg at the same time.

"Stop, or you'll break the egg!" cried Rory in alarm.

Flim jumped up at once.

"Oh!" she clucked in concern. "I hadn't thought of that."

But Flam just sat down on the egg and smiled. "I win!" she cried.

Rory cleared his throat. "Cock-a-doodle-do!" he crowed. "Flam, get off that egg. Flim cares about it more than you do, so from now on, it belongs to her."

"Wise Rory!" cheered the other hens, and they settled down on their nests for a peaceful sleep.

The Tale Of The Mer-Pig

Sometimes Edward the seagull would stop by the pigsty, and tell tales of the sea. Penny the pig loved to listen. She would gaze at the gull, her eyes glowing.

One night after a visit from Edward, she thought she heard a voice in her ear.

"Swim!" it whispered.

So Penny kicked her trotters. All at once she found herself under the sea, swimming beside another little pig – with a fish's tail!

"I'm a mer-pig," said the creature.

Together they explored the ocean, swimming with the fish and sending surprised crabs scuttling across the seabed.

"Now I must take you home," said the mer-pig. And she gave Penny a beautiful shell.

The next morning, Penny told her family all about her adventure, but they didn't believe her.

"There's no such thing as mer-pigs," they said.

Penny smiled and clutched her shell tightly. She knew better!

A Christmas Sledge Ride

For Christmas Finlay the turkey got a bright red sledge.

"Brilliant!" he gobbled excitedly. "What's it for?"

His mother smiled. "You carry it to the top of the hill and sit on it. Then you slide all the way to the bottom."

"Wow!" said Graham. And off he went to try it out.

An hour later, Finlay returned looking very cross. "It doesn't work!" he said.

"You silly turkey!" she laughed. "You need to wait for the snow first!"

That night, snow fell around the farm, covering the ground in a thick white blanket. Mrs Turkey took Finlay and his sledge to the top of the hill again. This time, when Finlay sat on his sledge, the slippery snow made the sledge slide.

"Wheeeee!" he yelled as he zoomed down to the bottom. "Can I do it again?"

How To Catch A Thief

The chickens were angry. Someone was stealing their grain.

"We must keep a watch to catch the thief," said the Colonel, the oldest cockerel on the farm.

That night, he and his son were patrolling the farmyard when they heard a scratching noise from behind some bags of grain.

"Quick," whispered the Colonel. "The thief is over there!" They pulled the bags out of the way and shone their torch in the corner. There, blinking in the light, was Hetty the hen, munching through a bowl of grain.

"I'm so hungry!" poor Hetty cried. "My brothers and sisters always gobble up the food before I get any."

The Colonel took Hetty back to her parents, and they promised that she could always eat her food before her brothers and sisters in future.

The Milkshake Cow

Lucy the cow was fed up with eating grass, especially when the farmer's strawberries looked so red and juicy. So she tiptoed across the farmyard and nibbled a few while no-one was looking.

"Look at my strawberry patch!" cried the farmer, when he saw what Lucy had done. "You've trampled it and turned my strawberries to nothing more than mush."

He collected all the crushed strawberries and put them in a bucket to make jam. Then he went inside to wash his hands.

Just then, the farmer's wife came out, picked up the bucket and began to milk Lucy. She didn't see the strawberries.

"Goodness!" she shrieked, looking in the bucket when she had finished. "Lucy has eaten so many strawberries, she's made strawberry milkshake!"

The farmer laughed and laughed. When he explained what had happened, his wife laughed too. As for the milkshake – it was delicious!

Just Like Old Times

Nell the old carthorse was telling her great granddaughter, Violet, all about the days when she pulled the hay cart and the plough on the farm.

"There were no tractors then," she said.

"I'd love to see the harness you wore, with all the ribbons and horsebrasses," said Violet. "You must have looked beautiful."

Nell smiled. "In a little while," she said.

Then one morning the farmer came and began to brush Nell's coat. Next, he dressed her in a jingling harness, and plaited her mane and tail with ribbons. She even had little caps over her ears to keep the flies away.

Violet watched in amazement. "Why are you dressed up?" she asked.

"It's the village show," replied Nell. "I'm in the parade – just like I have been every year since I was little. Come and watch!"

That afternoon, no-one was more proud of Nell than Violet was.

Mum Always Knows Best

The kittens' bedroom was a terrible mess. There were clothes everywhere, wet paintings and toys all over the floor so it was hard to find a clear space to walk!

"You really must keep your room more tidy," scolded Mrs Cat. "But there's no time to do anything about it now. You must get ready for Pepper the puppy's birthday party. It's almost time to go."

"We want to wear our new blue dresses with the pink ribbon," said the kittens. But they couldn't find them anywhere, no matter how hard they looked. The room was just too untidy.

Suddenly they caught sight of the pink ribbon under a pile of books. They pulled – and an old jam jar of water tipped all over their new dresses.

"What a shame!" said Mum. "You'll have to wear your old party dresses now. They'll suit you just as well."

The kittens looked sheepish. "Now we know why it's important to keep our room tidy," they meowed sadly.

Wheelbarrow Winners

It was Farm Fun Day, and the wheelbarrow race between the ducks and the pigs was about to begin.

The duck team were sure they would win. They had been practising for weeks. No-one knew the pigs' team had spread tractor grease all along the ducks' side of the racetrack.

The race began, and all the animals began cheering. The ducks' barrow was soon in the lead, when – DISASTER! Their barrow hit a patch of grease and went skidding into the pond. The pigs thought this was very funny … until they skidded on a grease patch too, and ended up in the pond as well!

The goats who were judging the race decided to call it a draw, so the prize – an enormous jar of sweets – was shared between the two teams – after the pigs had apologised for trying to cheat, of course!

The Runaway Guinea Pig

One day a strange-looking little animal appeared in the farmyard.

"I'm Gilly the guinea pig," she announced.

"You don't look much like a pig to me," said one of the geese. "What are you doing here?"

"I live in the house down the road," said Gilly, " but I've left home. Can I live here with all of you?"

Mrs Pig smiled. "Your mum will worry about you if you're away too long," she said. "But you can certainly come for tea with my piglets."

Gilly settled down to share the piglets' tea and Mrs Pig sent Billy the goat to fetch Gilly's mum.

It started to get dark on the farm, and Gilly felt very small. Then luckily her mum arrived.

"It's my mummy!" Gilly squeaked, snuggling up with her on Billy's back for the journey home. "I like the farm, but I think visiting is best," she said happily.

A Very Tight Squeeze

All the young animals on the farm were camping for the weekend with their teacher, Mr Gander. First they put up their tents. Then they gathered around the camping stove and tucked into big plates of beans and told campfire stories. Some of the stories were very scary – all about ghosts in the wood.

Later that night, Mr Gander heard a strange noise. So he poked his head through his tentflap and saw … a very strange shape sticking out of one of the tents.

"Who's that?" he cried, running over.

It was Boris the bullock. He was stuck half into the tent and couldn't get out.

"I was scared of ghosts," he explained to Mr Gander, after he had been rescued. "I was coming to find you!"

Mr Gander smiled.

"You're safe now, he smiled. "I'll keep a watch for any ghosts!"

Owen And The Apples

Owen the pig looked over the wall of his sty at the big red rosy apples hanging on the tree.

"Yum! Yum!" he sighed. "If only I could escape I'd eat those juicy apples." Just then, Milly the farmer's daughter arrived with a bucket of scraps for Owen's tea.

"It's your favourite," she smiled. "Potato chips, porridge and cornflakes."

"Harrumph," snorted Owen ungratefully, "I'd rather have some juicy apples. But he gobbled up every last scrap all the same.

Then Owen noticed that Milly had left the latch off the gate. He pushed the gate gently and it fell open.

"Yippee!" cried Owen, as he scurried over to the apple tree and began to gobble the juicy red apples. They were as tasty as they looked, and greedy Owen gobbled the whole lot! But … oh dear! What a terrible tummy ache he had that night!

Annie And The Mystery Egg

One day, Annie the hen found an egg hidden in the hay. Since no-one seemed to want it, she decided to take care of it herself.

A few days later, as Annie was sitting on the egg, she felt it move. She jumped up and watched as the egg cracked. Out popped a hungry chick!

Annie fed the chick with juicy worms. Soon, it was as big as Annie, and could flap its wings, as if it was trying to fly.

"Oh dear," said Annie. "I can't teach you. Hens can't fly. What am I to do?"

Then she had an idea. She went to the pond to ask the ducks for help. When they saw the chick they quacked and quacked! The little chick quacked right back. It was a baby duck!

Annie hugged the duckling. "You belong here with the ducks," she said, "but I'll visit you everyday, I promise!" And that's what she did.

Big Surprise At Bluebell Farm

A farm is always a busy place, but one week Bluebell Farm was even busier than usual. The sheds had been tidied, the gate mended, and all the animals were sweeping up.

"What's going on?" asked the baby animals, but their parents would only tell them it was a surprise.

"How can we find out what it is?" wondered the little ones.

"I know – I'll hide in the straw and listen to the horses," said Polly the puppy. But the straw made her sneeze, and the horses shooed her away. No matter what they tried, the baby animals couldn't discover the secret.

Finally, the big day arrived. There was an excited buzz in the air. "Ready?" said Farmer Barley to all the animals.

He opened the gates, and a stream of children skipped into the farmyard.

"Welcome to our Farm Open Day," chorused all the animals.

"What a brilliant surprise!" cheered the baby animals. "It was definitely worth waiting for!" and they played with the children all day long.

Snowy's Sneaky Snack

Snowy the lamb's aunt and uncle and cousin Woolly were coming for tea, and Snowy's mum had made a cake.

"Will they be here soon?" asked Snowy, eyeing the cake hungrily. At last, the doorbell rang. But the grown-ups wanted to chat before tea, so they sent Snowy and Woolly out to play. Snowy could see the cake through the window.

"I'm going to get a drink," she told Woolly, as she went into the kitchen. The cake looked SOOO wonderful.

"No-one will notice if I just take a nibble," Snowy thought. She popped a little piece in her mouth. It was delicious, so she had another nibble! Then she went back outside.

"Was it good?" asked Woolly.

"How did you guess?" asked Snowy in surprise.

"Easy!" laughed Woolly. "You've got crumbs on your lips. But I guessed that's what you went inside for. I would always test the cake first too!"

Christmas Decorations

It was almost Christmas, the snow was deep, and the young animals on the farm were very excited.

"Why don't you go sledging?" suggested their parents, who had lots of jobs to do. So Poppy and Penny the piglets got out their sledge, and everyone had a wonderful time taking turns to zoom down the high bank near the woods.

When everyone was all ready to set off for home, Ellen the lamb gave a shout.

"Look at that holly tree with lots of lovely red berries!" she cried. "Let's take some home on the sledge and decorate the barn for Christmas!"
And so they did. When the animals sat down for Christmas dinner, the grown-ups agreed they had never seen the barn look so pretty!

Benjamin And The Wasp

Benjamin the piglet was very proud of his curly tail.

"Your tail is straight and boring," he said to his friend Jamie the donkey. "It's not pretty and curly like mine."

"My tail is more useful," replied Jamie. But Benjamin just laughed. All at once, Wally the wasp buzzed past and stopped for a rest on Benjamin's back.

"Get off!" cried Benjamin, who didn't like wasps at all. And he shook Wally so roughly that the little wasp got angry and stung him.

"Ow!" cried Benjamin. "That hurt!" Wally the wasp then flew off and landed on Jamie's back.

"Let me have a comfy sleep on your back or I'll sting you too!" he threatened. SWISH! With one sweep of his tail, Jamie swept the grumpy wasp off his back. Wally was so surprised he flew away at once.

"I told you my tail was useful," laughed Jamie.

Lift Off For Little Monty

Mrs Duck had been taking her ducklings to the pond to practise their swimming every day, and they all loved it – except for Monty, that is.

"Why must I learn to swim?" he complained, refusing to get in the water. "I'd much rather stay dry."

"All ducks swim," said his mother, who was beginning to feel a bit impatient. But still Monty refused to put a foot in the water.

Now, it happened to be a very windy day, and as Monty waddled along by the side watching his brothers and sisters swim, a gust of wind caught his feathers, lifted him up … and dropped him in the pond! The water felt cool and silky all around him, and Monty found his webbed feet were already pushing him quickly towards the others. He took to it like … a duck to water!

"WOW!" he quacked. "This is fun! Maybe I will learn to swim after all!"

The Tale Of Two Tails

When Connie the carthorse met Pimpernel the pony, she was NOT impressed!

"Why, your head hardly reaches my shoulder!" she laughed.

"You don't have to be big to be useful," retorted Pimpernel, feeling offended.

So Connie went to one side of the field and Pimpernel to the other. And that is where they stayed all through the spring. Then came the hot weather … and the flies! All day long, the flies buzzed around Connie and Pimpernel at each end of the field. Both horses flicked at the bothersome bugs with their tails, but they just kept on coming …

Then Connie had an idea. "One tail isn't enough for all these flies," she neighed to Pimpernel.

"But two tails might work," said Pimpernel.

Soon the two horses were standing together, head to tail – the very best of friends – flicking their tails in turn, and batting the irritating flies all over the place!

Rufus And The Big Crash

Rufus the pig was sure he could drive the farmer's tractor.

"I've watched the farmer often enough," he said. "It looks easy!"

"Don't be silly," scoffed his friends. "Pigs don't drive tractors!"

But Rufus was determined to try.

One day, the farmer left his tractor in the yard with the engine running while he popped into the farmhouse. Rufus seized his chance. He leapt out of his sty and clambered into the cab, knocking a big lever as he did so. VROOM! went the tractor, and began to roll forward.

"Look! I'm driving!" called Rufus in delight. But his delight soon turned to horror. The tractor was heading for his pigsty, and Rufus didn't know how to stop it. CRASH! It hit the wall and knocked a big hole in it.

The farmer was furious. "You naughty pig!" he cried. "I hope that teaches you a lesson. Stick to what you're good at - being a pig!"

Where's My Bone Gone?

Patch had lost his favourite bone.

"I know I buried it here somewhere," he woofed, digging in the flowerbed. Then there was a shout. "You bad dog!" cried Mrs Plum, rushing over. "You've dug up my garden!"

Patch hid by the barn while Mrs Plum replanted her flowers.

"I'm sure I buried it in that flowerbed," he thought to himself. So he waited until Mrs Plum had gone, then sneaked back and began to dig again. Suddenly, he found something. Was it his bone? No, it was several things - hard and shiny, with a horrible taste of metal!

"You wicked dog!" shouted Mrs Plum, rushing over. "There'll be no more bones for …"

All of a sudden, she reached in the hole and picked up the hard shiny things. They were gold coins.

"Clever boy!" she cried. "You've found buried treasure! Who would have thought there'd be treasure in my back garden!" And she took the coins into the kitchen, giggling to herself.

Next morning she gave Patch his own treasure - the biggest, juiciest bone he had ever seen in his life!

Thomas To The Rescue

All the animals on the farm were enjoying a day at the seaside. The grown-ups sat in their deckchairs, the puppies chased off into the sea, and the lambs and kittens built sandcastles. Thomas the donkey gave everyone rides, the calves explored the rock pools and the piglets collected shells.

When everyone was hungry, Mrs Horse unpacked two huge picnic baskets, and they all sat down for lunch. Then the tide began to come in.

"It's time to go home," said the grown-ups, packing up. "Is everybody ready?"

They all nodded, except for the piglets.

"We've collected so many shells, they won't fit in our buckets," they oinked.

"Don't worry!" said Thomas. "Put your shells in the empty picnic baskets and tie them to my back. I can carry them back up the path to the bus." And he did just that!

The Look-Out Doves

The white doves hadn't lived on the farm for very long. The farmer had built them a wooden house – called a dovecote – high on the roof of the barn.

"How can we make friends with the other animals?" wondered the doves, as they sat up on the roof. Then they had an idea. Once a week a van delivered special animal food. When the doves saw it in the distance, they called out,

"The food van is on its way. Hurry across the field to your food troughs!"

The hungry animals rushed off to their troughs, and were waiting for the farmer when he arrived with their food.

"I think we have very clever animals," the farmer told his wife. "They seem to know what day of the week their food arrives."

And by doing this, the doves became part of the happy farmyard family!

Tabitha Has A Cold Bath

Tabitha the cat was sitting on the wall with her kittens.

"I'm going to teach you how to wash yourselves," she said. "Cats like to be clean, but it takes a bit of practice, so watch me."

Three of her four kittens did as they were told, but the fourth called Tiger had other ideas. He'd seen two birds splashing in a puddle having a bath. "That looks fun," he meowed. "I think I'll try that."

He leapt off the wall and landed in the puddle with a SPLASH!

"Oh! It's cold!" he squealed. "My fur is wet and my tail is soggy!"

"You silly kitten," laughed his mother. "Cat's don't like getting wet!"

"Then how can I take a bath?" asked Tiger.

"Cat's don't take a bath!" his mother smiled. "They lick their fur clean. Now watch me, and I'll start the lesson again!"

Betty The Bat Has A Guest

Betty the bat slept all day, but at night she flew around the farm, visiting her friends. One windy evening she dropped by to see her friend Cordelia the sparrow. But when she arrived Cordelia's nest was nowhere to be found.

"What am I to do?" cried Cordelia. "The wind has blown my nest away."

"Don't worry," said Betty, "You can come home with me tonight."

"But what if the wind has blown away your nest too?" worried Cordelia. Betty just smiled.

Betty and Cordelia flew back to Betty's home - a large solid wooden barn! They flew high into the beams beneath the roof.

"We'll be quite safe here," said Betty, hanging upside down. Cordelia snuggled up on a beam beside her, warm and dry and safe. And though the wind whistled and roared all night, it didn't worry them one bit!

Penelope And The Moon

One evening Penelope the pig lay on her back looking at the Moon.

"I wonder what the Moon is?" she thought. Then she asked Molly the cow.

"That's easy – it's a huge bucket of creamy milk," replied Molly.

Charlotte the sheep disagreed. "It's a giant ball of white wool," she said firmly. Now Penelope was really confused, so she asked her friend Henrietta the hen, who was generally very clever, what she thought the Moon was.

"It's obvious, isn't it?" clucked Henrietta. "It's a big white egg."

By now, Penelope didn't know what to think, so she decided to ask her mother.

"Who is telling the truth?" she asked.

"They are all telling the truth," replied her mother wisely. "Since none of us really know what the Moon is, it can be whatever we want it to be. What would you like it to be?"

Penelope thought long and hard, rubbed her chin and said, "A large, soft, creamy cheese, ripe and ready for me to eat!"

"Well, there you are then!" said her mother.

What would YOU like the Moon to be?

Farmyard Rock 'n' Roll

Libby the lamb wanted to start a band.

"But we haven't got any musical instruments," laughed her friend Sammy the calf.

"We can make our own," cried Libby. She jumped on an old oil drum and danced around, making a loud drumming noise. Then she jumped on a bigger drum that made a different, deeper sound. "There, I'm the drummer!" she sang. Sammy blew into some long plastic pipes, and made a loud honking sound.

"What's all the noise?" asked Henry the hedgehog, rustling through the dry leaves under the hedge.

"Hey! That rustling sounds great!" laughed Libby. "Come and join our band." Soon Archie the goat had joined in too, plucking the wire on the fence to sound like a guitar.

When everyone played the instruments together, they sounded just like a real band, and the other farm animals just couldn't resist dancing.

"I think we're a hit!" cried Libby.

The First Day At School

Twins Rosie and Clover were starting school, and they were very nervous. They had never met their new teacher Mrs Turkey, but they had often seen her in the farmyard. She had black beady eyes, a wrinkly neck, and a habit of appearing whenever someone was doing something they shouldn't.

"Do you think she will be a grumpy teacher?" whispered Rosie, as they ran into their new classroom.

"VERY grumpy!" replied Clover. "We'd better try to be good."

Rosie and Clover sat down with their new classmates while Mrs Turkey sat in the corner, writing. Then she looked up with her beady black eyes … and smiled the kindest smile.

"Hello class," she said in a gentle voice. "I think you all know me, I'm Mrs Turkey. I just know we're all going to get on really well."
Rosie and Clover breathed a deep sigh and relaxed in their chairs.

"Everything's going to be all right after all," grinned Rosie. And do you know, she was right!

A Billion Bouncy Balls

Ruben the rabbit had a new ball. It was red rubber, and very bouncy!

"Ouch!" bleated Jake the goat, when it bounced on his head.

"Go and play somewhere else," squawked the hens, when it bounced through the barn and woke them up.

"Bother!" said Ruben. And he took his ball to the very edge of the farmyard. This time he bounced it so high that it bounced and bounced, till it vanished over the farmyard wall. Ruben scurried under the fence and looked around. He couldn't see his ball anywhere. Then he looked up. He could not believe his eyes. Wherever he looked, there were trees, and each tree were covered in red balls!

"How will I ever know which one is mine?" he wailed.

"You silly rabbit," laughed Jessica Squirrel. "These are apples, and this is an orchard. Try looking for your ball on the ground."

And sure enough, that was where Ruben found his bright red bouncy rubber ball.

Ginger The Guard Cat

Every night Ginger the cat went round the farm to check on all the animals. The hens thought this was hilarious. "She thinks she's a guard dog!" they giggled when Ginger wasn't listening.

One night, Ginger was doing her rounds as usual. She visited Gregory the goat, Drummer the pony, and then made her way to the henhouse.

"Is everything all right?" she called.

But everything wasn't all right. The lock on the henhouse door was broken, and Fergus the Fox was trying to get in.

Ginger raced back to the farmhouse.

"Help!" she meowed loudly. The farmer woke up at once and ran to the henhouse – just in time to chase the fox away.

"Thank you for saving our chicks, Ginger!" clucked the grateful hens. "You are as brave as a real guard dog." And they never made fun of Ginger again.

There's No Place Like Home!

Luke, the farmer's son, had two rabbits called Nibbles and Nutmeg. They lived in a hutch by the farmhouse, and he fed them everyday with crisp lettuce and dandelion leaves. Then he would let them out for a run in a big pen he had made.

One night, some wild rabbits crept up to the hutch and called out,

"Why don't you two escape and come to live with us?" they whispered. "We're not shut in a rotten old hutch. We're free!"

Nibbles and Nutmeg looked at each other. "No thank you," said Nibbles. "We have a warm house with clean straw to lie in." "And we have fresh food and a run every day," added Nutmeg.

So the visitors hopped off to their burrow, leaving the two pet rabbits behind. "There's no place like home!" agreed Nibbles and Nutmeg.